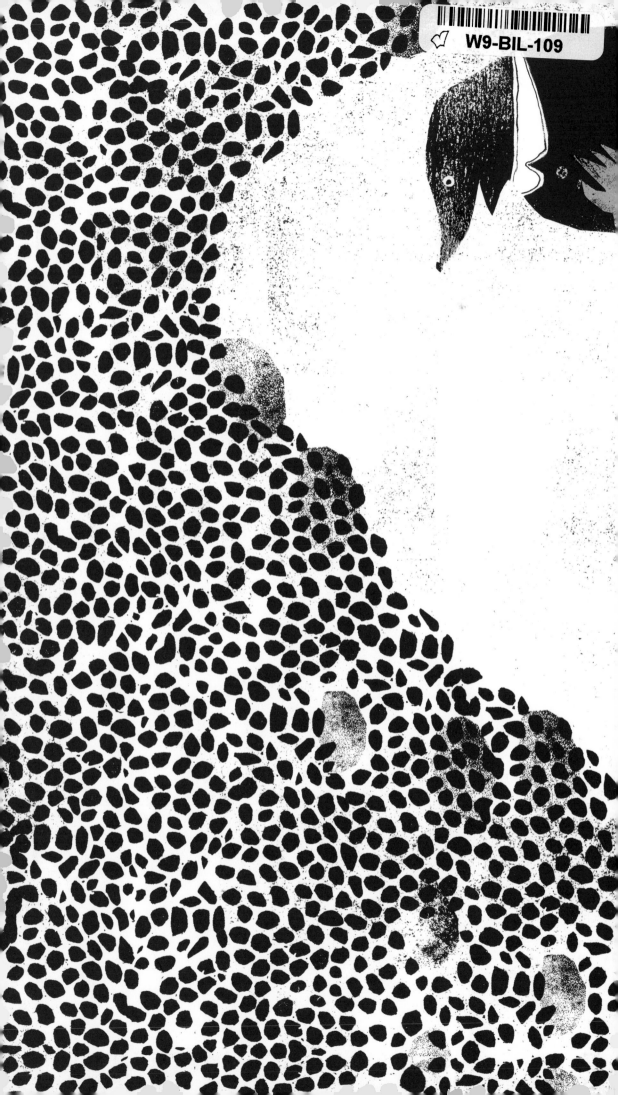

Mole in a Black & White Hole

Tereza Sediva

Mole in a Black & White Hole

For Lévi & Vilma
You color my world – T.S.

Mole lived in a hole, deep under the ground.

It was dark and it was damp but it was his home.

He lived alone apart from his only friend,
a bright pink chandelier.

Mole found great comfort in chatting to his friend and loved how colorful he was.

Sometimes he wondered if there might be more out there if he looked. But he was too scared to leave his little hole.

Mole tried to be brave. He would scrabble through the earth as far as the nearest worm (who made him jump) but then he'd go straight back to his hole and his friend.

It was all he'd ever known.

Chandelier tried to persuade him to go further.

"There is so much color and so much life to be found. But to find it, you must search for it," he would say to Mole.

"There are blossoming trees and blooming flowers, I can see it all with my leaves."

Mole wasn't sure, "All year round?" he asked suspiciously. "Do they never change?"

"Of course," said Chandelier. "The golden sun turns the flowers into glossy fruits for the colorful birds to eat."

"What happens when the fruit has all gone?" asked Mole. "What does the sun shine on then?"

"The sun can always find something to shine on. Sometimes there are clothes as colorful as the rainbow drying outside."

Mole looked down at his furry black
coat and sighed.

"The sun makes everything look beautiful."

"The houses in town sparkle with color when the sun comes out."

«El sol debe estar agotado de tanto brillar», dijo Topo.

«Bueno, también está la luna que cuando se encuentra con el sol, este se pone muy tímido. Se sonroja y tiñe todo de color rosado y naranjo antes de esconderse durante toda la noche», afirmó Lamparilla.

«Y luego todo vuelve al blanco y negro», exclamó Topo, con gran satisfacción.

Al día siguiente, Topo despertó con
un rayo de sol cálido en la mejilla.
Cuando abrió los ojos, no podía ver
nada; había demasiada luz.

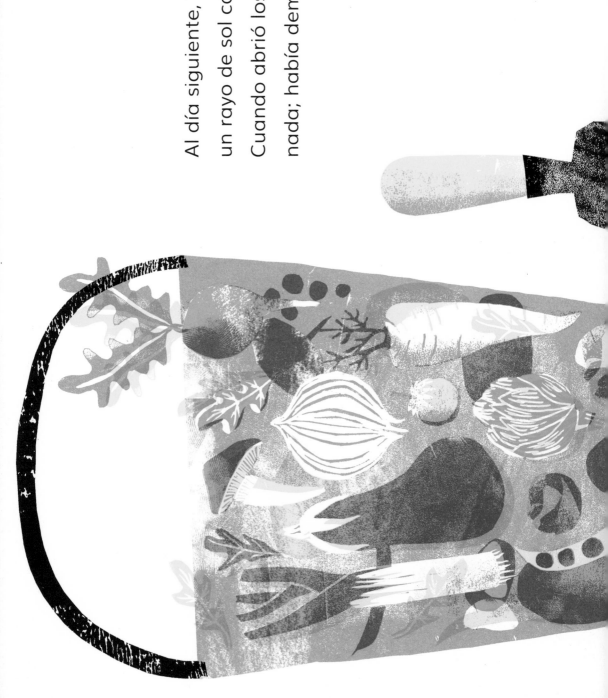

Había tanta luz que, por unos momentos, no se dio cuenta de qué faltaba…

¡Su querida Lamparilla no estaba!

En ese instante su mundo pareció más oscuro y negro que nunca.

Lloró y lloró y lloró hasta que se le acabaron las lágrimas.

Pero luego recordó las palabras de su amiga...

«Si quiero encontrar color, debo buscarlo».

Buscó debajo de las piedras pequeñas
y también de las más grandes.

Buscó debajo de su manta.

Cavó hacia abajo y cavó hacia el lado...

And eventually when there was nowhere else to go he decided to be brave and go up, through the hole where his friend had been.

When he popped his head out of the hole he got a surprise.

The night was not black and white like he had thought....

The silver moon shined like a precious jewel and in the
town the windows gleamed and lit up the night.

Mole gazed in awe!

Then the dawn came up and the world became a glorious riot of color. It wasn't just color, it was a world full of wonder.

The birds sang and the scent of the flowers filled the air. Mole felt so alive. It was very different from his dark little hole.

Mole had a very good idea.
He looked around and
gathered up some
colorful things.

Back in his hole, Mole found that
life was not so black and white and
lonely anymore.

"Now, I can have color down here and up there," he said happily.

He had the best of both worlds. His cozy colorful hole and this whole new world full of friends to explore.

Special thanks to my husband, my dad, Martin,
Roger and Anna for helping Mole out into the world.

Mole in a Black and White Hole © 2021 Thames & Hudson Ltd

Text and illustrations © 2021 Tereza Sediva

First published in 2021 in the United States of America by
Thames & Hudson Inc., 500 Fifth Avenue, New York, New York 10110

Library of Congress Control Number 2020931196

ISBN 978-0-500-65205-3

Printed and bound in China by Reliance Printing (Shenzhen) Co. Ltd

Be the first to know about our new releases,
exclusive content and author events by visiting
thamesandhudson.com
thamesandhudsonusa.com
thamesandhudson.com.au

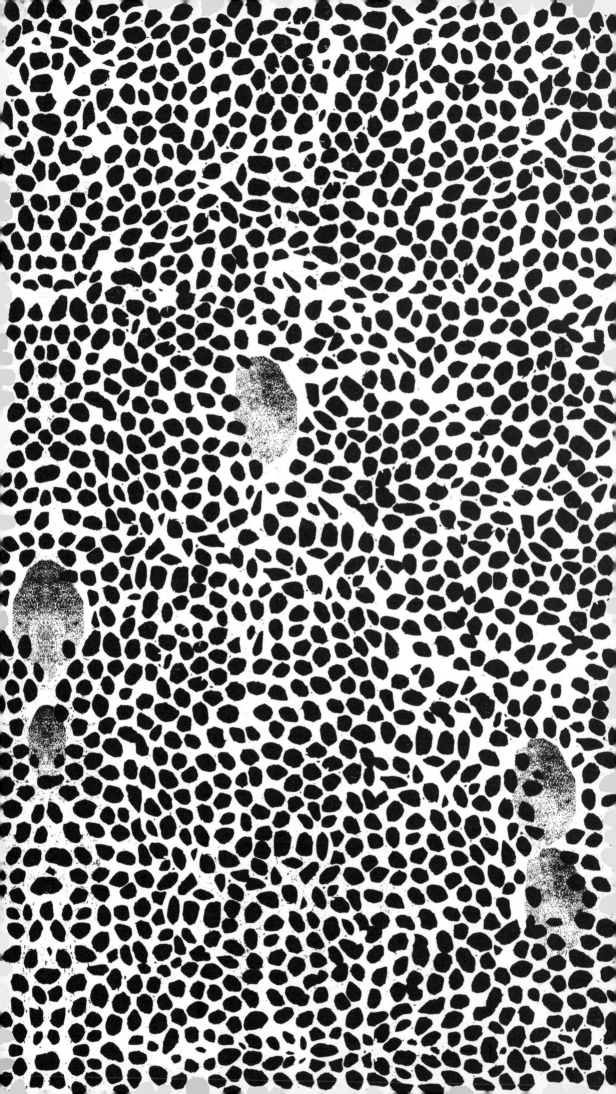